★ How ★
★ BRAVE
Is ★ That?

Anne Fine

How BRAVE Is That?

with illustrations by
Vicki Gausden

Barrington Stoke

First published in 2013 in Great Britain by
Barrington Stoke Ltd
18 Walker Street, Edinburgh, EH3 7LP

www.barringtonstoke.co.uk

Reprinted 2014, 2015

A CIP catalogue record for this book is available
from the British Library upon request

ISBN: 978-1-78112-243-3

Printed in China by Leo

Contents

Chapter 1

Ta-ta-*ta-ta-ta-ta!* *Ta-ta-ta-ta-ta-ta!*

Tom wants to join the *army*. He always has. Back when we were in nursery he'd head for the dressing-up box, root about till he found the soldier's cap, and ram it on his head. He'd pick up anything to use as a gun. They didn't let us play with proper toy guns in nursery.

Once Tom picked up Safira's doll and pointed it at the wall. "Ta-ta-ta-ta-ta-ta," he shouted. "You're dead! You're all dead!"

Safira began to cry. Miss Lane made Tom give the doll back and say sorry.

"How can I join the army," Tom said, "if I don't learn to shoot?"

"No shooting in here!" said Miss Lane. "Only outside."

So when we were outside, that's what we did. We played at being soldiers. I used to get bored. (I don't want to join the army, like Tom. I want to look after forest trees, like my dad. Or run a café, like my mum.)

But that's all Tom wanted to do, and Tom's my friend. So we played soldiers with pretend guns.

We were still doing it when we moved up to primary school. On the first day, Mrs Dell gave us all some pencils and a ruler made of wood. Tom got a magic marker and he blacked out bits along the side of his ruler.

"What are you doing?" I asked.

Tom held it up. He'd made his ruler look as if it was a long, slim gun. It even looked as if it had a trigger.

"Do mine as well," I begged him.

So he did.

"Ace!" I said. As soon as the buzzer rang for break, we ran out into the playground. We crawled around and hid from made-up enemies and pretended to shoot back when they shot at us.

"Quick! Here they come again!"

"Ta-ta-*ta-ta-ta-ta! Ta-ta-ta-ta-ta-ta!*"

Mrs Dell heard the noise and asked what we were doing. Tom hid his ruler gun behind his back.

"Gary and I are just going round the playground measuring things with our new rulers," he said.

"That's not true, is it?" said Mrs Dell. "That would be a *quiet* thing to do, and you are making more noise than anyone else in this playground."

Tom hung his head.

"Now show me what you've got hidden behind your back," said Mrs Dell.

So Tom held out his ruler. It was all smudged from being held so tight. Tom's hands were black as well.

"Oh, Tom!" said Mrs Dell. "What a horrid mess you've made of that lovely new ruler."

"I have to practise shooting," Tom explained. "You see, when I'm old enough I want to join the army."

Mrs Dell looked stern. "If you want to join the army, Tom, you'll have to be brave," she said. "And brave people tell the *truth*."

After she'd turned away, Tom stuck his tongue out at her back. But I think what she said fixed in his brain because from that day on, Tom never, ever told a lie.

Chapter 2

No Good at Lessons

Tom was no good at lessons. He was slow at reading and he got stuck on almost all the long words. His writing was terrible. It looked as if a spider had got drunk and danced across the page. Even I couldn't read what he wrote, and I sat next to him, so I was used to all his back-to-front letters and his messy rubbings out.

At home, his mum sat by his side to help him get things done, and he had extra help in school.

"I have to try to get it right," he said. "I'll have to pass exams to get in the army."

I asked my dad if that was true. "Yes," he said. "Tom will have to be able to read labels. He'll have to read the instructions for all of the fancy equipment. He'll have to be able to write clear messages."

"I hadn't thought of that," I said. "I suppose I had the idea that soldiers just shoot at people and get shot at back."

My dad gave me a look. "Then I think we can all be grateful you're not planning on joining the army," he said.

"I'm not that brave," I said. "If someone started to fire guns at me, I'd run like crazy, but the other way."

My dad grinned. "As I said, we must be grateful you have other plans."

Chapter 3

Say That Again and I'll *Thump* You

Then we moved up to the big school. Everything changed. We had a different teacher for each subject, and sometimes Tom and I were put in different classrooms.

Each teacher had his or her own way of doing things, but they were all the same in one way.

They were all dead fussed about school uniform.

If you walked round with your shirt flapping, they'd be on top of you in a moment. "Tuck in that shirt, please!"

If your tie was loose round your neck, they'd nag at you. "Do up that tie, please!"

If you wore trainers, you were in big trouble. I was sent home to change once, so I never made the same mistake again. And my mate Arif lives about a thousand miles away from school. So he once went round for the whole day in socks rather than go home and change.

I don't know why the teachers were so strict about it all, but they were.

The school was fine in other ways. We went on lots of trips. We did school plays. There was a lot of football. For the first year or two, Tom still had extra help from a lady called Mrs Pratt, and she was lovely. Tom even got into a fight about her once. I saw him at the gates with a black eye.

I pointed. "How did you get that?"

"Alan punched me."

"Why?"

Tom blushed. "Because I punched him first."

"But he's the size of a *barn*. Why did you do that?"

"Well," Tom told me, "Alan said something that I didn't like, so I said, 'Say that again and I'll *thump* you'."

"And Alan said it again?"

"Yes."

"So you thumped him? Even though Alan's ten metres tall and solid as a hippopotamus?"

"I had to, didn't I? I'd said I would if he said it again. And then he said it."

"*What?*"

Tom blushed. "He said that Mrs Pratt was a prat."

"You got into a fight to defend Mrs Pratt?"

"Why not?" he said.

And later, when I thought about it, it made sense. After all, Tom wants to join the army. And armies often spend their time defending people who can't get in fights themselves.

So sticking up for Mrs Pratt was probably good practice for Tom's career plans.

(Not to mention brave.)

Chapter 4

Then Something Terrible Happened

Then something terrible happened.

Tom's mum had triplets.

That's right. Three babies. All at the same time.

One moment Tom is walking round, an only child like me. The next, he has three baby sisters.

They all looked the same to me. (Sometimes all pink and sleepy. Sometimes red-faced and screaming.)

Tom said he could tell them apart. I used to test him. "Which one is Milly?"

He'd point to one of them. "That one. That's Milly."

"How do you *know*?"

"Easy," he said. "She's a bit fatter than Tilly and she hasn't got quite as much hair as Gilly."

"She looks *exactly the same*," I said. "They *all* do. All three of them look *exactly the same*."

"No, they don't."

"Yes, they do."

We must have spent hours arguing about it because we spent hours looking after them. We'd look after Tilly and Milly while Tom's mum took Gilly to the doctor. Or we'd look after Milly and Gilly while Tilly was asleep and Tom's mum took a quick shower. Or we'd feed Gilly and Tilly while Tom's mum trimmed Milly's finger nails.

It was all right while they were babies.

But then they grew a bit, and caused more trouble. Tom came to school one day in a bright yellow shirt.

Mr Simms stopped him in the corridor. "Tom," he said. "On the day that the school uniform changes from white shirts to bright yellow shirts, I will be sure to let you know. But right now, all pupils wear white shirts. So why are you sporting this buttercup yellow number?"

"There wasn't anything else," Tom said. "Milly threw up on one of my white shirts, and after I changed, Tilly threw up on the other."

Everyone knew about the triplets.

"Oh," Mr Simms said. "Oh, I see."

We think he must have had small babies once himself, because he didn't say another word, and strolled off whistling.

Chapter 5

What are Those Horrible Things on Your Feet?

A few days later, Tom came in wearing ratty blue trainers.

Mrs Day pounced on him. "What are those horrible things on your feet? Where are your plain black shoes?"

Tom hung his head. "I've no idea," he said. "Tilly was playing with one of them, then it vanished."

"How can a shoe just vanish?" Mrs Day asked.

"I don't know," Tom said. "Mum and I looked everywhere. Everywhere!"

Mrs Day was irritated. "It must be somewhere," she said.

Tom was irritated too. "That's what Mum keeps on saying," he told her. "She keeps on saying, 'Your shoe must be *somewhere*, Tom!' But it isn't! I don't believe I'll ever find it again."

Tom wore his ratty blue trainers for four whole days. But then his dad came home from working on the oil rig. That meant there were enough grown ups in the house to have a proper fire and keep everyone safe – even with the triplets about. And that was how Tom's shoe was found again. It turned out that Tilly had taken lots of bits of coal out of the coal box and stuffed some of them one-by-one into Tom's shoe. Once it was full, she'd put the shoe into the coal box and dumped more coal back on top.

"I should have *thought*," said Tom's mum after his dad had snatched the shoe back from the fire just in time. "I had to hoover up all the coal dust twice. I should have *thought*."

Tom's very kind to his mum. "It's not your fault," he told her. "It's the school's own fault for making us wear coal black shoes."

Chapter 6
Puffy Clown Trousers

Another good week passed. Then Tom came in on Monday morning wearing puffy clown trousers with purple zig-zag stripes and giant red spots.

I met him in the entrance hall. "Wow!" I said. "There can't be many people with the guts to come to school in stuff from their old dressing-up box."

"No choice," he told me gloomily. "Mr Simms said I can't afford to miss a single maths lesson if I'm to pass the exam."

I gave the puffy clown pants another look. "I think I'd rather stay at home and fail."

"I can't," said Tom. "Not if I want to join the army. And I do."

Then Mrs Hicks came round the corner and saw Tom. She wasn't happy. "Is this a *school*?" she scolded. "Or a circus tent? How dare you come in here looking like that?"

"I'm sorry," Tom said. "But I had to wear these, or not come at all. You see, Gilly stood up for the first time today, and she pulled the plastic baby bath off the stand. So all the water fell on the washing pile and my only dry pair of school trousers got soaking wet."

Mrs Hicks scowled. "You could at least have put on something more sensible – even a pair of dark jeans."

"I don't have any jeans," said Tom. "Tilly has chewed a big hole in them. Somewhere important. Mum says they're not fit to wear but she hasn't had the time to sew them up because of the triplets."

"Can't you mend them yourself?"

"No," Tom said. "Dad's back on the oil rig now, so as soon as I get home I have to look after Milly and Gilly and Tilly while Mum has a shower."

"That's true," I said. "I've been there. All we do is look after Tilly and Gilly and Milly. They can't do anything for themselves."

"Except be sick, and hide my shoes and chew through my clothes," Tom muttered.

"Except be sick and hide Tom's shoes and chew through his clothes," I said so Mrs Hicks could hear.

Mrs Hicks sighed. "This can't go on," she said to Tom. "We can't be patient forever. School rules are school rules. And you must know that if Mrs Bell catches you, you'll be in the worst trouble."

Mrs Bell is our head teacher. She is world famous for fussing about uniform.

And for her temper.

"So, Tom," said Mrs Hicks, "however difficult things are at home, you'll have to make more of an effort to come each day in the right clothes."

"I will," said Tom.

And he went off to his first class in his clown trousers with the purple zig-zag stripes and big red spots.

I thought that was pretty brave.

Chapter 7
Gilly? Milly? Tilly?

That was all nothing compared to what happened next. It was a few weeks later, on the morning of a pretty important maths exam.

I waited for Tom at the gates. To be fair, he wasn't looking all that odd when he arrived. He had on one of his dad's striped shirts, some dark green jeans and grubby tennis shoes. If he'd been mooching round the shops on Saturday morning, no one would have looked at him twice.

I plucked at the not-proper-uniform striped shirt. "Gilly?"

"No," he said. "Tilly. She pulled off her dirty nappy and left it upside down on my pile of school shirts."

I pointed to the not-proper-uniform dark green jeans. "Milly?"

"Gilly," he said. "She stuffed my school trousers into the washing basket, and Mum threw them into the machine by mistake. They were still sloshing round as I left home."

I nodded at the not-proper-uniform grubby tennis shoes. "Tilly?"

"No," he said. "Milly. She crawled out into the garden with my school shoes and we haven't seen them since. I think that next door's dog has buried them somewhere."

"I'd lend you what I'm wearing," I said. "Except that I have to do this exam as well. And if I don't, my mum and dad will kill me."

Tom knows my mum and dad, so he just nodded.

"Let's creep through the lunch hall," I said. "At least that way we can get round to the exam room without going past Mrs Bell's office."

Chapter 8

The Worst Luck

We had the worst luck.

Just as we reached the end of the last corridor, Mrs Bell swept round the corner in full sail.

She took one look at Tom and she went mad. "Don't even think that you can go in that room dressed like that! It's out of the question! You must be wearing proper uniform to sit an exam in this school. So just go home and change!"

"I can't!" wailed Tom. "All of my things are covered in baby mess, or soaking wet, or buried in a hole!"

Mrs Bell wasn't listening. "This is a school and we have rules! You are not going in that room unless you are in proper uniform!" She pointed to the front door. "Go home and change! Right now!"

"But I want to join the *army*!" Tom howled. "So this exam's *important*. And it starts in *three minutes*!"

Mrs Bell didn't even hear. She'd swept into the room and left the two of us standing outside.

Chapter 9

Go Boil Your Head!

Tom went dead white. I thought that he was going to cry. People were hurrying past us into the exam room. Only two minutes left!

I couldn't bear to leave him.

Just then, Lucy Brown came out of the girls' changing rooms dressed in her netball gear – a short-sleeved shirt and flappy grey shorts. Lucy lives three doors down from me. She's two years older, but I know her well.

I had a sudden idea.

"Quick, Lucy!" I said. "Lend us all your clothes."

"Go boil your head!" said Lucy.

"No," I said. "I mean it! Tom here needs to take an exam. Right this minute! And Mrs Bell won't let him in the room unless he's in proper uniform. And you've got proper uniform in there, just sitting in a locker, doing nothing. So lend it to him, just till break."

Lucy stared at us both. "You're joking! Aren't you?"

"No, I'm not!" I said. "If Tom is brave enough to join the army, then he must be brave enough to wear a skirt."

Already I was busy helping Tom unbutton his striped shirt. "Please, Lucy! Please!" I begged.

She saw that we were serious. "Oh, all right, then! But just till break!"

"Yes, just till break! I promise!"

So Tom ripped off the striped shirt and scrambled out of his dark green jeans while Lucy rushed back to her locker to get her stuff. Then he climbed into Lucy's skirt. It wouldn't do up, but the blouse and jersey hid the bit of Tom's skin that showed.

Lucy's shoes were far too small. But Mr Simms was walking down the corridor – in plain black shoes.

So I stopped him as well.

"Please, sir! Please, sir! Can you swap shoes with Tom, just until break? You see, Mrs Bell won't let him take the maths exam unless he's wearing proper uniform."

Mr Simms hasn't spent three years nursing poor Tom through every maths class for nothing. I've never seen a man take off his shoes so fast.

He looked at the grubby tennis shoes that Tom held out in exchange.

"Not sure I fancy those," he said at last. "I think I'll manage until break."

And he went off in his red socks, whistling cheerfully.

I grabbed Tom's arm. "Come on! They're starting! Hurry up!"

Chapter 10

How Brave is *That?*

It takes true grit and a backbone of steel to march into a room wearing a skirt. (If you're a boy, that is.)

Everyone laughed. Some people jeered. Some people hooted. Some giggled.

Lots of the boys wolf-whistled as Tom strode by.

"Nice combo," Ruth sniggered.

"Give us a twirl," begged Safira.

"Brave fashion choice!" said Dean.

Then Mrs Bell saw him. Maybe she'd had time to think twice. Or maybe Mrs Day had managed to remind her about the triplets. Perhaps she'd just decided she wouldn't tangle with Tom again.

After all, he was wearing proper school uniform. (No argument about that.)

So Mrs Bell just rapped the desk and everyone went quiet. Then she and Mrs Day gave out papers as we all watched the clock hand tick its slow way through the last minute before the exam began.

"Right," Mrs Bell said. "Go!"

We all picked up our pens and pencils and began.

Tom passed. (And so did I.)

Mr Simms got his shoes back. Tom's mum bought Lucy a big box of chocolates to thank her. (I got one as well, for my quick wits.)

Mrs Hicks told me I should think of joining the army too, along with Tom. "They need smart thinkers," she said.

"No way!" I said. "I haven't got the sort of guts you need to be a soldier. I couldn't walk into a room wearing a skirt!"

I mean, for heaven's sake! How brave is *that*?

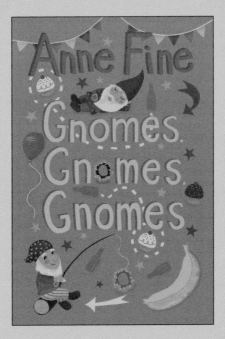

Sam's a bit obsessed. Any time he gets his
hands on some clay, he makes gnomes. Dozens and
dozens and dozens of gnomes.

Funny thing is, Sam doesn't like to have gnomes in
his room. So they live huddled together, out in the shed.

But when Sam's mum suddenly needs that space,
she says the gnomes will have to go. And so Sam plans
a send-off for his little clay friends – a send-off that
turns into a night the family will never forget!

'A superb and subtle writer' MAL PEET, THE GUARDIAN

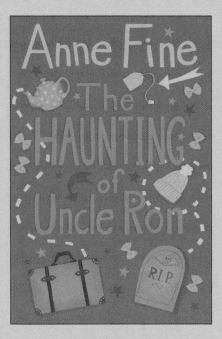

Ian thinks the new girl next door looks amazing.
But he's not so keen on Uncle Ron, the world's most
boring visitor.

Even the voices Uncle Ron hears from the 'Other Side'
have nothing interesting to say. On and on they go
about missing socks and blue underpants, while Uncle
Ron feasts on non-stop snacks.

Ian can't stand it a moment longer.
He must get rid of Uncle Ron. What he needs is
a plan – and perhaps a helper ...

'A superb and subtle writer' MAL PEET, THE GUARDIAN

More **4u2read** titles ...

All Sorts to Make a World
JOHN AGARD

Shona's day has been packed with characters. First there was 3.2-million-year-old Lucy in the Natural History Museum, and then Pinstripe Man, Kindle Woman, Doctor Bananas and the iPod Twins.

Now Shona and her dad are on a Tube train that's stuck in a tunnel and everyone around them is going ... bananas.

Hostage
MALORIE BLACKMAN

"I'll make sure your dad never sees you again!"

Blindfolded. Alone. Angela has no idea where she is or what will happen next. The only thing she knows is she's been kidnapped. Is she brave enough to escape?

Nadine Dreams of Home
BERNARD ASHLEY

Nadine finds Britain real scary. Not scary like soldiers, or burning buildings, or the sound of guns. But scary in other ways. If only her father were here. But it's just Nadine, her mother and her little brother now. They have no idea if they will ever see Nadine's father again. But then Nadine finds a special picture and dreams a special dream ...

Deadly Letter
MARY HOFFMAN

"Ip dip sky blue. Who's it? Not you."

Prity wants to play with the other children at school, but it's hard when you're the new girl and you don't know the rules. And it doesn't help when you're saddled with a name that sounds like a joke.

Will Prity ever fit in?

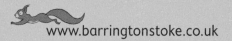

www.barringtonstoke.co.uk